Fangs-giving

Rojin

Fangs-giving

Dian Curtis Regan

AN
APPLE
PAPERBACK

SCHOLASTIC INC.
New York Toronto London Auckland Sydney

ISBN 0-590-96821-1

12 11 10 9 8 7 6 5 4 3 2   7 8 9/9 0 1/0

Printed in the U.S.A.   40

First Scholastic printing, November 1996

For the POD
That prestigious group who brightens
my days — and nights.
Beware of chupacabras and orcas with fangs.

Contents

1.
To Grandmother's House We Go

"**O**ver the river and through the woods to Grandmother's house we go — "

Whap!

"Ouch!"

Matthew Kubat tried to keep a straight face as Rosie, his little sister, whipped around to glare at him in the backseat.

"Dad, Matt threw something at me."

Widening his eyes, Matt tried to look clueless as he caught his father's tired gaze in the rearview mirror.

"Ki-ids," was all Dad said.

"It hurt," grumped Rosie.

How could a gum wrapper hurt? Matt wondered.

The wrapper didn't hurt, his mind pointed out. *The wad of already chewed gum inside did.*

Oh, right.

Matt settled back to watch scenery flash past the windows of his dad's Jeep. Late afternoon was quickly dimming into evening on this cold November day.

He felt sorry for the goats scattered across the hillside, and hoped they had a cozy barn waiting at nightfall.

As tired as he was of hearing Rosie sing the "Over the river" song, Matt had to admit the words *did* describe the road they'd turned onto from the main highway out of Thorndale.

After crossing several bridges, the Jeep wove through an ever-thickening forest. *Cool*, Matt thought, glad Mom had sent them with Dad for Thanksgiving weekend so they could tromp to the country to stay at Grandma Kubat's new house.

Suddenly the Jeep swerved, sending everyone sliding to the left, then right as Dad recovered.

"Pothole," he muttered, fumbling with the map. "Can't believe your grandmother bought a home in the boondocks. How's she supposed to run to the store for a carton of milk?"

Matt figured it'd be fun to live in the boondocks — as long as he still had cable TV, Super Nintendo, and Internet access. And his friends lived nearby. *And* the arcade and theater and mall were down the street.

Then it wouldn't be the boondocks.

Oh, right.

"Son, help me with this." Dad tossed a map over the seat. "We turned off the highway on

2

Burgess Road. Seems like we should have come to Calumet by now."

Matt held the map close to the window to take advantage of the fading daylight. He spotted a line of ink arrows Dad had drawn while on the phone last night, getting directions from Grandma. "Have we passed Hazard Creek?" He liked the sound of the name.

"Mmm — " Dad began.

"Yes," Rosie blurted. "That was the last bridge because it reminded me of . . . Over the river and through the woods, to Grandmother's — "

Whap!

That was the folded-up map meeting the top of Rosie's curly head.

"Ouch!"

"Ki-ids. . . ."

Unrolling the map, Matt traced the ink arrows with his finger, searching for Calumet Road. "Here it is. Four bridges after the turn."

Dad slowed for a sharp curve. "One more to go then. Keep your eyes peeled. It's getting hard to read signs."

"A bridge!" Rosie hollered, making Matt jump.

"Number four," Dad exclaimed. "Good job, Eagle-eye."

"And there's the turnoff for Calumet," Matt added, not wanting Rosie to ace him out of being the official Kubat family navigator.

The Jeep lurched and bounced around a bend, then barreled up a rocky rise.

"Wanna play a game?" Rosie asked. "Count the potholes?"

"No." Matt groaned. Why did she have to turn everything into a game? Or a song?

After a few more winding curves, Dad steered the Jeep up a gravel drive and parked in front of a rustic, multilevel house, painted in earth tones.

Beep! Beep!

Grandma dashed out the front door and down a long wooden stairway to the drive. She wore a sweater and broomstick skirt, covered by a paint-smudged apron that read, "Queen of my Castle."

Climbing from the Jeep, there were hugs all around, and comments like: "You've grown since summer!" (To Matt.) "Where are your two front teeth?" (To Rosie.) "What do you think of my new digs?" (To Dad.)

All three studied the house, carved into the forest as if it were trying to hide from the main road.

"Did you have to move so far from civilization?" Dad teased.

"Barry, dear, I'm an artist. I need space and quiet to create my sculptures."

"But, Mother — "

4

"I have a neighbor now. Down the road. Old Mr. Pryor. He's raised a turkey for Thanksgiving and wants the kids to come have a look at it."

Ewww. Matt immediately felt sorry for the poor turkey.

"Come inside," Grandma urged. "Can't wait to show off my house and studio." Opening her arms, she herded them toward the wooden steps.

"I'll get the bags," Matt offered, ducking under her arm.

He wanted to lag behind because he thought he'd seen something move through the shadowed pines along the side of the house.

A dog? He couldn't imagine his grandmother getting a pet since she traveled so much. Must be a stray. Maybe he could make friends with it. At least it'd give him something to do during his holiday "in the boondocks."

Matt carried two suitcases up the stairs, plopped them onto the cedar porch by the door, then headed back after his own.

Hoisting his bag over one shoulder, he slammed the door of the Jeep shut and hurried into the trees beside the house. "Here, boy," Matt called, whistling softly. "Come out so I can see you."

Matt stepped deeper into the grove of pines. Hard to see anything. The moon was on the rise, but didn't offer much light through heavy clouds.

He felt sure the dog was still around. He could almost sense its presence, like it was huddled behind a fat spruce tree, watching him.

Letting his bag slide to the ground, Matt ventured ahead, clicking his tongue and snapping his fingers.

"Rats," he finally mumbled. "So, you're playing hard to get. I'm *only* trying to be friendly." He paused, listening for rustling leaves, but the wind teased his ears by rustling leaves in all directions.

"Okay for now, but I'll be back with food; I'll bet you're hungry." Hesitating, he added, "Funny. I *know* you're here. I can feel — "

Whomp!

It was not a dog Matt felt.

Rather, a hand.

A large, firm hand.

Clamping down painfully hard on his shoulder.

2.
Strangers in the Night

Shock froze Matt, muffling his scream into a whimper.

Twisting free, he raced toward a light — a Chinese lantern on the back deck. Dodging trees, he locked his gaze onto the glow, willing it to save him from whoever or whatever had grabbed him.

Afraid to listen for pounding footsteps behind him, Matt leaped up the back stairs and lunged for the glass door.

It slid open effortlessly.

Why wasn't the door locked? Sure, he was grateful, but didn't his grandmother know strangers lurked in Calumet Woods?

Matt slammed the door and flipped the lock into place.

Panting, he leaned his forehead against the cold glass and peered out. In the lantern's glare, he couldn't see beyond the deck railing.

He felt along the wall with both hands until his

fingers located the switch and clicked off the light.

Darkness spread across the trees like syrup coating the branches.

No monster stood on the deck.

No wild animal moved through the moonlit trees below.

Did I imagine it?

No! Matt rubbed his shoulder, still feeling the iron grip of . . . whatever.

Giving up, he yanked a drape across the glass door and turned on a lamp. Brightness chased the bogeyman from the room — and his imagination.

He stood in a cozy den with a sofa, a TV that wasn't plugged in yet, and lots of bookcases. The shelves held scattered books and grandma knick-knacks. Crates and boxes bordered the room. She obviously hadn't finished moving in yet.

Voices drew Matt from the den toward the front of the house. Rosie flew around a corner, hugging her suitcase to her chest. "This one, Grandma?" she hollered.

Grandma peeked around the corner. "Yes, that's your room. I put Lamb Baby on the bed for you. Wiggly Walrus is in your brother's room."

Matt cringed at Grandma's embarrassing words. Rosie had a thing for lambs. Her room at home was done in "lamb motif."

Him? He'd outgrown that beat-up walrus *loooong* ago. Yet, after tonight's near-brush with doom, somehow knowing Wiggly Walrus was within reach was *very* comforting — although he'd never admit it out loud.

"Matthew, there you are." Grandma straightened his hair the way grandmothers do. "Come see my living room. Then you can put your things in the den." She disappeared around the corner.

His things? Oh, no. He'd left his bag outside with that . . . that nightmare. No way was he going after it. Let it sit beneath a tree till morning. He'd sleep in his clothes and overlook brushing his teeth.

Matt followed her to the living room — a loft overlooking the entryway.

Pine walls, hung with Native American rugs, glowed warmly in the soft light. The high ceiling was criss-crossed with beams. Windows sprang from ground level, rising all the way to the ceiling.

Matt assumed the view during the day was awesome. But at night, those windows were black, gaping holes — with nary a curtain in sight.

Whoever had accosted him in the yard now had a wonderful view of the living room.

And him.

Matt backed into the shadows, tripping over something on the floor.

His bag! How did it get here?

Dad and Grandma finished chatting (arguing?) about the long trip to Calumet Woods.

"Matthew, you must have already found the den since you came in the back," Grandma said. "That will be your room. After dinner, we'll turn the sofa into a bed."

Matt was still staring at his bag.

"You left it outside, dear. Hagerty brought it in."

"Hagerty?"

From a dark doorway stepped a man so tall, he had to stoop to keep from bumping his head. "You called, Ma'am?"

"Here's the other grandchild I wanted you to meet," Grandma said. "This is Matthew, and he's in sixth grade."

Matt stared at the giant of a man. His hair, longish and uncombed, was black with a white streak on one side. His face was pale, and he was so thin, his shirt hung loose on his wiry frame.

Plus, he wore dark glasses, which Matt found exceedingly odd.

Dad nudged him. "Where are your manners, Son?"

"H-hello," Matt said, shooting his father a perplexed frown.

"Hagerty is your grandmother's handyman," Dad explained. "He's helping her move in, hang pictures, arrange furniture. That sort of thing."

Matt could tell by his dad's too-smooth tone that the appearance of a stranger in Grandma's house wasn't sitting too well with him, either.

"Not only a handyman, but a wonderful cook — and errand runner," Grandma chirped. "He's been such a help to me. Hagerty, please put Matthew's bag in the den. I can't wait to take my guests on a quick tour of the studio. Give us ten minutes, then we'll be down for dinner."

Hagerty nodded, moving to fetch the bag.

The pale hand that reached for the luggage strap held Matt's attention. It was the largest hand he'd ever seen. It was the hand that had clamped down on his shoulder outside in the dark trees — he was sure of it.

He was just trying to help you.

Of course.

Matt desperately wanted to agree with his inner voice.

Then he glanced at Hagerty's face.

The man peered at him over the top of his dark glasses. A smirk twisted the corners of his mouth.

He knows, Matt thought. *He knows he scared the jelly beans out of me.*

Their gazes locked. The man was obviously amused.

And he *knows that* I *know.*

Rosie dashed through the room to follow Dad

and Grandma upstairs to the studio. Matt moved quickly after them.

As for Grandma's handyman, cook, errand runner — or whoever the guy was supposed to be — Matt planned on keeping a fair distance from this strange stranger with the even stranger name.

3.
Things Look Better in the Morning

Matt woke, instantly confused over where he was.

Oh, right. The den in Grandma's new house.

Stretching, he thought about last night's tour of her studio: slabs of clay for sculpting, a kiln, paints, tarps for the floor. And, dominating the room, the yucky smell of turpentine left over from an afternoon project.

Although his grandmother's taste in art was different from his (she liked flowers; he liked spacecraft), Matt was proud of her. She had even been commissioned to design a sculpture for Thorndale Park.

After the studio tour, dinner had been squash soup with sourdough bread (which tasted better than it sounded).

Then off to bed — and the nightmare that troubled his sleep.

Matt sat up. Wait a minute. That was no nightmare. His moment of terror last night had been real.

Shuddering, he remembered the handyman — Hagerty — and his puzzling gaze. Luckily, the man had left dinner on the table last night and disappeared before the family sat down to eat.

Scrambling from bed, Matt yanked aside the curtains. Bright sun beamed on a small clearing in the backyard, bordered by the forest. Patches of snow lingered from the last storm.

The sky was a glorious blue. Matt grinned at the view and the promise of a fun day exploring the woods and the streams they'd crossed on the way in.

And, tonight, a hearty Thanksgiving dinner: turkey, cranberry sauce, bread pudding, pumpkin pie with two mountains of whipped cream.

Mmm. He could hardly wait.

The door burst open and Rosie tumbled into the room. Her curls lay flat on one side from sleeping. Her lamb pajamas (lamb-jamas to her) dusted the floor. "Get up. It's time for breakfast."

Matt glared at her. "As you can plainly see, I'm already up. Don't you ever knock?"

"Grandma told me to wake you," she proclaimed, as if it gave her authority over closed doors. "We're eating breakfast while she's gone."

"Gone?" A vague uneasiness tingled through him. He did *not* want to be left alone in the house with that weird person. "Is Dad still here?"

Rosie shot him a curious look. "Of course. Grandma just went jogging."

"Jogging?" Somehow the words *jogging* and *Grandma* didn't fit together in his mind.

"Hurry," Rosie told him. "Hagerty made peach waffles with pecans."

Hagerty and *peach waffles* didn't fit together either.

"Leave," Matt ordered. "So I can get dressed." Out she went, slamming the door.

"Little sisters," Matt griped. "Bah humbug."

Breakfast was, in fact, delicious. Hagerty served waffles until they could eat no more. He was quiet and efficient, moving around the kitchen like a shadow, barely noticeable.

He still wore dark glasses, even though the curtains were closed and the kitchen was far from bright. This morning, he also wore gloves.

What a mysterious dude, Matt thought.

Dad, too, was quiet, reaching around the *Thorndale Times* for his coffee or to snitch pumpkin muffins.

Rosie chattered to Hagerty — about Lamb Baby, who'd joined them for breakfast, how much she liked Mrs. Alvarado, her first-grade teacher, how Christmas was only twenty-seven days away, and how she hoped Mom or Dad or SOMEBODY remembered how much she wanted a *real* lamb.

Hagerty nodded politely, as if truly interested in listening to a six-year-old babble on about herself.

Matt kicked her under the table. She was embarrassing him.

"Ouch."

"You're not getting a lamb for Christmas. Where are we supposed to keep it?"

"In my room."

"Yeah, right. Tell that to Mom."

"Dad, Matt kicked me and said I couldn't keep a lamb in my room."

"Ki-ids." Dad turned a page and reached for another muffin.

"So, can I have a real lamb for Christmas?" Rosie asked.

"Mm-mmm."

"Seeeee?" Rosie made a face at Matt.

Hagerty snickered. Matt's sentiments exactly.

He glanced at the man. Maybe Hagerty wasn't so bad. Maybe they just got off on the wrong foot. Everything seemed much more normal here in the kitchen by the light of day.

"I'm ba-ack!" came Grandma's voice from the entryway.

Seconds later, she burst into the kitchen, wearing a pink and purple running outfit, which matched her shoes and headband.

What had gotten into his grandmother?

"I did three miles," she huffed. "With old Mr.

Pryor. Except he couldn't keep up because he was disturbed about his turkey. Something got it in the middle of the night. He found it dead this morning, with these funny marks on its neck."

"Your herbal tea, Ma'am," Hagerty said, pulling out a chair for her.

Grandma grabbed a booklet from a drawer and joined them at the table. She slid the book toward Matt. "The realtor who sold me the house gave me this. It's a book of local legends. Fun to read. Thought you could do a report on the stories for school."

Matt glanced at the contents. "The Mysterious *Chupacabras*," "Legend of the Vampire Cave," and "Secrets of Calumet Woods" quickly caught his attention. He liked reading stuff like this.

"Wow, thanks," he said, wondering what *chupacabras* meant.

Matt studied the picture on the cover. A bat flew from the top left corner of the illustration, slowly transforming into a man by the time it landed on the lower right side. A man wearing a cape. Sporting fangs from his half smile. A vampire.

Cool.

Scooting back his chair, Matt bumped into something.

Hagerty.

"Oops, sorry."

The man had been reading over his shoulder.

After acting so aloof, why the sudden interest?

Matt excused himself. "I'm going outside for a while."

"Take your sister."

"Awwwww."

Dad folded the paper and set it on the table. "You'll have to keep an eye on her, Son. It would be too easy for her to wander off into the forest."

Rosie stopped drinking orange juice long enough to wrinkle her nose. "I'm almost seven, you know."

Matt scoffed. "Yeah, in eleven more months."

Grandma chuckled. "You two tiff just like your father and his sister did. It's so cute. Isn't it cute, Barry?"

Dad wrinkled his nose like Rosie. "I don't recall your thinking it cute while it was happening twenty-five years ago." He tweaked Grandma's cheek to show he was kidding.

Ignoring him, she patted Matt's arm. "My Barry and Belinda were the cutest toddlers you ever saw."

Matt and Rosie laughed. Hard to imagine Dad and Aunt Belinda as toddlers.

"Okay, Sis, come on." Matt tried to act nicer so his father would have pleasant memories of *them* in twenty-five years.

"I'm not finished eating," Rosie said. "And I'm not going outside in my lamb-jamas."

"Fine." Matt dumped his dishes into the sink.

"Meet me in the backyard when you're ready."

He glanced at Hagerty. The man had been staring at him ever since Grandma set the booklet on the table. Why?

He has an interest in local legends. Don't make a big deal out of it.

Okay, okay.

Matt reaaaaallly wanted to agree with the logic of his inner voice — yet his gut instincts were telling him a completely different story.

4.
Hide and Shriek

Matt perched on the bottom step of the back deck to wait for Rosie.

The sun shone brightly — but not warmly. A zippy breeze made him button his jacket and pull up the hood.

Matt's grandmother amazed him — not because she'd bought this mountain home, not because she'd jogged three miles in the frigid morning air, but because she'd saved the spooky booklet for him to read.

His mother would have yelped, "Oh, Matthew — ick! Can't you find something better to read?"

Eagerly opening to the first story, he read a legend about a group of campers who stumbled across a vampire cave back in the 1970s. Only one camper escaped to tell a tale of underground caverns inhabited by vampires en route to other stops around the world.

The story reminded Matt of the "Underground Railroad" from the 1800s. Was this an underground hideout for creatures of the night? Ha!

No one believed the outrageous story told by the camper who escaped. Many wanted him to stand trial for the disappearance of his friends, but no one could show evidence that a crime had been committed.

The chapter on *chupacabras* was *really* interesting. Over the years, small animals in Calumet Woods had been found dead, with fang marks on their necks.

The stories were connected to a similar legend from Puerto Rico, only there, the victims were mostly goats. *Chupacabras* actually translated into "goat-suckers."

Yikes.

Matt was fascinated.

Then he remembered his grandmother's words about Mr. Pryor's poor turkey. "Something got it in the middle of the night."

What else had she said? "Mr. Pryor found it dead this morning, with these funny marks on its neck."

Yikes, yikes, yikes.

Those stories happened a long time ago, Kubat, and they're legends, meaning, nobody knows whether or not they're true.

"Ready?!"

Matt was so deeply immersed in mental images of a turkey coming face-to-face with a *chupacabra* (chupa-turkey?) that his sister's abrupt holler made him slide off the step and plop onto the hard, frozen ground.

"Ouch!"

Rosie clomped down the steps, clearly pleased at how much she'd startled him. "Let's play hide-and-seek!" she cried, leaping over him and dashing off into the trees. "You're It!"

"Wait!" Matt scrambled to his feet. Normally, he'd let her go — and good riddance. But after Dad's command to watch out for her, coupled with the gory stuff he'd just read, his big-brother conscience kicked in.

He tore after her.

"Stop, Rosie!" Matt called. "Don't you want to go exploring instead?"

"I want to play games," she hollered back, not even slowing. Topping a hill, she disappeared down the other side.

Groan. She was going through her first-grade "Let's play games!" stage, interchanged with her "Let's sing songs!" phase.

Matt glanced back toward the house to get his bearings. Only the tip of the chimney could be seen above the pines. Sighing, he hustled after his sister, mentally noting the direction they were hiking.

Why did she have to be so headstrong? And why couldn't she stick to the path that wove across the clearing and into the woods instead of dashing helter skelter over wooded hill and dale?

"Rosie!" Matt shouted. "Hold up! You're gonna get lost and I won't be able to find you!"

He braced himself for her gibberish reply about how she was almost seven and too old to get lost.

He didn't brace himself for the reply that came instead. . . .

Silence.

Followed by a shriek.

A high-pitched, hair-raising, little-sister kind of shriek.

5.
Poor Lamb Baby

"Ro — !" Matt shouted, but the rest of her name lodged in his throat.

He scrambled up a rise, frantic. What had happened to her? All he could think about were those bridges they'd crossed yesterday.

What if she'd fallen into a stream? It would be his fault. He'd let her get away from him. He . . .

There she was, huddled by a boulder iced with snow.

Matt hopped over tangled underbrush and slid through frozen mush to get to her.

Rosie gazed up at him. Tears streaked her face.

"What happened?" Matt huffed, out of breath. "Did you fall?"

"Lamb Baby," she gasped between sobs.

"Lamb Baby? You brought him along from Grandma's? Did you drop him in the snow? Did you lose him?"

Whew, is that all? he added to himself. "We can find him," Matt assured her. "We'll just backtrack and retrace our steps to the house."

"No!" Rosie blurted. "Lamb Baby is dead."

"Huh?" Was this a new game?

Coming to her feet, Rosie motioned for him to follow.

Confused, Matt let her lead him around the boulder.

"Poor Lamb Baby," Rosie whispered in a voice full of tears.

Matt peeked around an outcropping of rocks. A goat — a *real* goat — lay on its side in the mud. Hadn't been there very long, and, in fact, looked as though it were taking a nap. The goat's fur matched the patches of snow surrounding it.

Matt moved closer, kneeling beside the animal. His gaze fell on what he'd feared to find: two marks in the goat's neck, with a smidgen of blood.

Chupacabras!

His heart pounded faster than it had when Rosie shrieked. Why had he read that booklet?

Still — better to be informed than —

"Hello," boomed a deep voice.

"Hi!" squeaked Rosie, sounding delighted.

From behind the rocks, Matt quickly took stock of the situation:

- A dead animal.
- A stranger in the forest.
- The possibility that they were lost.

Not good, his mind warned. *Not good.*

Rosie was jabbering away about "poor dead Lamb Baby."

Matt stepped around the boulder to see who she was talking to.

Hagerty.

Outside, he seemed even taller. Gloved hands clutched a walking stick with a carved bat on the top. The hood of Hagerty's cloak was pulled down to his dark glasses.

Sunlight hitting the lenses reflected Matt's mistrusting expression back at him. "What are you doing here?" he asked.

Hagerty studied both of them. "The question should be, what are *you* two doing here?"

Matt shrugged. "Exploring."

"That's how I found Lamb — "

"Hush, Rosie. It's not a lamb; it's a goat."

"Oh, poor child." Hagerty's voice sounded harmless and caring. "Animals stalk other animals. It's a law of nature. You mustn't be sad about losing one goat. Many others in the herd got away. Survival of the fittest rules out here in the wild."

A good explanation, Matt thought, although he

wondered how Hagerty knew about the "rest of the herd getting away."

"Come with me," the man continued, giving a slight bow. "The woods up a ways are beautiful this time of year. And the fabulous view from the bridge is — "

"No, thank you," Matt interrupted, then added politely, "we should be getting back to the house."

"Why?" asked Rosie. "We just left. I thought you wanted to go exploring."

Thanks, Sis.

"And exploring you shall go." Hagerty shuffled his boots, crumbling the crunchy snow beneath his feet. "Follow me on a quick tour — and I'll have you in for lunch."

"Yay!" sang Rosie, scuttling after him.

Matt watched her go, looking tiny as she tailed the taller-than-normal man. *Geez.* How quickly she'd accepted the fate of the dead goat.

Sighing, he couldn't come up with a good reason for not tagging along. After all, Hagerty lived in these woods; he knew his way around. Besides, now that an adult was escorting them, Matt wouldn't have to keep such a tight rein on Rosie.

Kicking at the gnarly root of a naked oak tree, Matt gave in, trudging around the boulder to follow. He couldn't resist a backward glance at the poor dead goat-baby.

Matt caught his breath.

The goat was gone.

27

6.
No More Games

They hiked for a loooooong time. Rosie had to sprint to keep up with Hagerty's lengthy strides.

Matt lagged behind.

The cautionary tale of Hansel and Gretel kept tapping him on the shoulder, making him post mental tags onto the scenery so they could find their way home. He was too smart to mark their way with bread crumbs, yet if he had any, he'd gobble them up to quell the rumblings in his stomach.

But Hagerty promised to have you "in for lunch."

Oh, yeah.

Why was it so hard to trust this guy? Grandma trusted him.

Finally, they burst out of the trees into a cozy meadow. Hagerty stepped briskly over a bridge spanning a frosty stream, then climbed a steep hill, and disappeared into the woods on the far side of the clearing.

Rosie loped across the wooden bridge and scampered up the hill.

Matt stopped in the middle to lean against the railing. Chunks of ice floated in the stream like tiny icebergs. *Brrrr.* Made him shiver.

Plunging cold hands deep into his pockets, he squinted at the sky. The sun was hiding behind clouds now, and didn't look as if it had any intention of reappearing for the rest of the day.

Matt wondered if this was the "fabulous view from the bridge" Hagerty had promised. All he could see were trees and more trees — some topped with snow, many with bare branches. All looked stiff and dead against the dull November sky.

"Say!" Matt hollered. "Mister, um, I mean, Hagerty?! Wait up!"

If this isn't the bridge he wanted to show us, I have a right to know how much farther we have to hike.

Matt's stomach grumbled again. So much for getting back in time for lunch.

Hagerty didn't respond to the call — or reappear.

Annoyed, Matt watched the dark trees swallow Rosie as she dashed to follow their tour guide.

"Rats."

He pictured a plate of sandwiches waiting in Grandma's kitchen, with her usual Thanksgiving warning of "Don't eat too much for lunch. Save yourself for dinner with all the trimmings."

He always ate too much, but it never stopped him from wolfing down her mouth-watering holiday supper. No way.

Giving up, he trudged off the bridge and headed after his sister.

At the top of the hill, Matt faltered. Trees grew so close together, he had to maneuver sideways to slip between some of them. It seemed darker and colder in this part of the forest.

"Rosie?" he called. "Hagerty?"

No answer.

Matt heated up. Where was his sister?

Why did I trust that man? What has he done with her?

Hagerty was probably so tired of listening to Rosie go on about herself and her teacher and her class and her Lamb Baby, he'd offered her a fat pinecone to munch so she'd stop chattering — ha!

"Rosie, answer me!" Matt demanded.

In the ensuing silence, a twig cracked somewhere behind him.

Hair on the back of his neck rose. "Come on, this isn't funny!"

Whap!

"You're It!"

Rosie danced around him, giggling her toothless giggle.

Matt's shocked heart began to beat again. "Don't do that!"

Grabbing Rosie, he mussed her hair until she wiggled away.

"You're It; you're It; you're It," she singsonged.

"When am I *not* It?" he asked in a bored voice. "No more games, Rosie. We could really get lost out here."

Matt glanced around. "Speaking of which — where did Hagerty go?"

"He told me to close my eyes and count to twenty, but I tricked him and only counted to fifteen." Lifting her chin, Rosie gave her brother a smug look.

"Well, aren't you clever?" Matt rolled his eyes. "What were you supposed to do on the count of twenty?"

"Whoops!" she exclaimed, as if she'd forgotten the rest of the game. "I'm supposed to look for him in that direction." She pointed toward a gloomy grove of evergreens.

"He told you which way to look?"

She nodded.

Matt *hoped* Hagerty had pointed out the correct direction to keep Rosie from dashing off and truly getting lost.

31

"I've got a better idea," he said, quickly changing Hagerty's plan. "Let's head back to Grandma's house."

Rosie wrinkled her nose. "Not yet."

"Aren't you hungry?"

"Sorta."

"Then let's go home and eat. We can explore again after lunch. I promise."

Inside, he knew he wouldn't wander this far into the forest again without a map or compass — or bread crumbs.

His sister defiantly crossed her arms. "No."

"Ro-sie, Grandma and Dad will be worried if we don't show up for lunch. Besides, Mom promised to call this afternoon, and we'll miss her."

Rosie kicked at a decaying tree stump. "Well, okay."

Finally, she listened to reason.

Relief at being rid of Hagerty made Matt feel almost giddy. "I'll race you down the hill to the bridge."

He took off, glancing behind at his sister.

She was running, too — but in the opposite direction.

Matt skidded on a patch of mud as he tried to stop. "RO-SIE! It's *this* way!"

"I'm coming!" she hollered back. "Just as soon as I tag Hagerty!"

7.
A Twist to the Plan

"Noooooo," Matt groaned. The whole point of this was to get *away* from Hagerty and back where everything seemed normal.

No dead animals, no weird strangers popping out of the trees. No one making them go on a hike deeper into the forest.

Matt dashed after his sister. If she refused to stop, then he'd scoop her up and carry her down to the bridge and back through Calumet Woods to familiar territory.

He was gaining on her. So close, he could see each curl bobbing against her head.

Swwwwooooooooshhhhhhhhhhh!

Stunned, Matt skidded to a stop.

ROSIE HAD DISAPPEARED!

One minute she was running — right in front of him, her feet pounding the ground and kicking up soggy leaves and dirt.

The next instant, the forest floor opened up

and swallowed her whole! Like the jaws of an underground dragon.

Matt panted, too shocked to catch his breath.

He tiptoed close to the spot where he'd last seen her.

Leaves and branches hid a hole dug deep into the earth. Rosie had stepped on the wrong place and. . . .

Ohmigosh! Panic fuzzed Matt's mind. Was this an animal trap? Was his sister caught in a pit with a wild — ?

"M-M-Matt?" The whimpery voice echoed against the earthen walls of the pit.

"Rosie?" He let out the breath he'd been holding. "What happened? Are you all right?"

"I fell into a hole."

"No kidding. Tell me you're okay." He hated this new game they were playing. Hated the twist to his plan. "Please?"

"I-I'm o-o-kay."

He could tell by her stuttering she was terrified.

"I'll get you out," Matt promised, inching closer. *How* he was going to get her out wasn't clear in his mind.

What about Hagerty? Where was he? He could help.

Matt glanced around, now annoyed with the guy for disappearing.

Dropping onto his stomach, he belly-swam

across the dirt to the lip of the hole. First things first. How deep was it? Maybe he could pull her out.

Matt peered over the edge.

Rosie gaped up at him, open-mouthed.

The look of horror on her face was one he'd never seen. He knew she was afraid of the dark. Every outlet in her bedroom at home sported a lamb night-light.

Twelve feet max, Matt calculated. Not *too* deep.

"Hang on, Sis," he told her. "I'm going to find a sturdy branch for you to grab hold of. Then I'll lift you out."

"O-o-kay."

"I'm moving out of sight now," he said to reassure her. "Keep talking to me." Rising onto his hands and knees, he backed away from the edge. "I'm right here. Can you still hear me?"

"Y-yes."

As Matt started to get up, the ground beneath him fell away.

Not the edge of the hole, but the entire piece of earth on which he was hunched, opened up and sucked him in.

Wind rushed past his ears as he plummeted.

Thump! Bump!

Landing hard, he shielded his face from falling dirt clumps.

After the earth stopped raining on him, he opened his eyes.

Rosie, looking petrified, hovered above him.

Beyond her head, a shadow moved past the tree-rimmed sky.

Hagerty! He'd come to save them.

But before Matt could scramble to his feet, before he could even shout the man's name, the earth above them closed — *whomp!* — like a steel trapdoor.

And the pit was thrown into utter darkness.

8.
Down the Rabbit Hole

The slamming of the trapdoor reverberated loudly in Matt's ears, broken only by the sound of Rosie's whimpers.

Or were they *his* whimpers?

Matt shoved himself up off the damp ground, feeling wobbly. The complete blackout had thrown off his sense of balance.

Rosie's arms went around his waist so tightly he could scarcely breathe. Still, he hugged her back.

How could he comfort his sister? Who was going to comfort *him*? Who would say, "It's going to be all right"?

"It's going to be all right," he heard himself whispering — only because he felt, as the older Kubat, those were words he was supposed to say.

"What's happening?" Rosie's voice was like a tiny bird peeping. Matt could barely hear her, even this close.

"I-I don't know," he began, "but — "

Shhhhhhhhhhhhhh!

"What's that?" she rasped.

"We're moving." Matt planted his feet wide to maintain balance as the entire pit plunged downward, like an earthen elevator. His fascination almost conquered his terror. How could this be happening?

The sensation of falling slowly down a hole suddenly reminded him of *Alice in Wonderland.*

"Hey, Rosie, let's play a game. Let's pretend you're Alice and you're falling down the rabbit hole."

"Really?"

Good thinking. Keep Rosie from freaking out and it will keep you from doing the same.

"Yeah. You're going to have lots of, um, adventures before you go home again." *Before you wake up and find out this is all a dream,* his mind added.

If this IS a dream, please let me wake up!

Ka-chunk!

The pit stopped moving.

"N-now what?" Rosie whisper-cried.

Matt wanted to tell her it was time for the Mad Hatter's tea party, but bickering voices on the other side of the wall took his words away.

Arguing?

So, people are down here.

Plus, rabbits and Cheshire cats and playing cards that can talk.

38

Quit fooling yourself, Kubat, you **KNOW** *what's down here.*

Vampires.

And now — you and Rosie.

In a trance, Matt watched the side of the pit crack and begin to open. Just like elevator doors.

Closing his eyes, he clutched his little sister and prepared for the worst.

9.
What Waited at the Bottom

"**H**agerty!"
Matt felt Rosie pull away. His eyes flew open just in time to see her dash from the pit into Hagerty's waiting arms.

So. The man could *not* be trusted. Matt had sensed it all along.

"There, there," Hagerty cooed, patting Rosie's shoulder while giving Matt a trickster sort of grin.

How could Rosie be so dense? How could she think this man was her friend?

Matt leaped from the pit, worried that the door might slam and he'd be taken deeper underground, separated from his sister.

He found himself in a small cavern. The aroma of moist dirt filled his senses. Figures lurked in the shadows, but Matt couldn't see them clearly.

Muted lamps along the walls glowed dimly with a soft reddish light.

Light in a vampire cave? *Mmm.* Matt was confused. Didn't vampires prefer the dark? Perhaps moving around in total blackness was just as difficult for them as it was for humans.

Blinking, he adjusted to the eeriness of the cave.

Rosie's thumb disappeared into her mouth. Matt hadn't seen her suck her thumb in years, but somehow he didn't blame her.

He turned his attention to Hagerty. Now the man wore all black, including a cape with a stand-up collar. Matt glared at him. "What do you want from us?" He hated the way his voice quivered in fear.

Hagerty unwound Rosie's grasp and shoved her into Matt.

Astonishment leaped onto her face, as if she couldn't believe Hagerty would treat her like that. Her jaw dropped as she gaped at him.

"What do we want from you?" the handyman-turned-vampire repeated. He motioned toward the faceless forms in the shadows. "We've been discussing just that."

Hagerty tapped a finger against one cheek. "What shall we do with a lad and lass who've learned of our existence?"

At first, Matt had no idea what Hagerty meant. Then he remembered Grandma's booklet and its cover illustration for "Legend of the Vampire Cave."

Matt scoffed. "You mean the book at

41

Grandma's house? I'll bet *hundreds* of people have read that booklet by now. What are you going to do? Round up all of them?"

Hagerty sucked in a breath. "Hundreds of people? What do you mean?"

Arguments buzzed from every dark corner of the cavern.

Matt shrugged. "The booklet is probably for sale at every store and gas station surrounding Calumet Woods."

Hagerty's face grew even paler. "Excuse me." He melted into the shadows to discuss this startling news with his colleagues.

"Rats, Rosie," Matt whispered. "Hagerty brought us here because he saw me reading Grandma's booklet."

In the red glow, hope flickered across his sister's face. "Is he going to take us home now?"

"Nooooo." Matt shook her by the shoulders. "Sis, this guy is *not* your friend. He's a . . . a . . ." Matt couldn't bring himself to call the guy a *chupacabra*, but how could he make Rosie understand? "You can't trust him. He's a mean person, and he plans to keep us here." *Or worse*, Matt's mind added.

"But what about Thanksgiving dinner?"

Geez. Making it back for Thanksgiving was the *least* of their worries right now. "We're going to miss dinner," Matt told her. He only hoped *they* didn't become somebody else's dinner. . . .

Rosie's face crinkled the way it always did before she burst into tears.

Hagerty stepped back into the lamplight. The red glow reflected menacingly in his eyes.

Matt had a brief, but brilliant brainstorm. "Hag, er, sir, er, Hagerty," he began, fumbling for words. "About the booklet. Rosie didn't read the story. She knows nothing about the vam . . . um, I mean, let her go. She hasn't done anything to threaten the existence of the cave."

Good thinking, Kubat. Hagerty will let Rosie go. She'll run home and tell Dad. He'll call the cops, and they'll tear out to Calumet Woods with fifty squad cars, sirens blaring, to rescue you. Just like in the movies.

"No!"

Hagerty's fierce retort put a quick end to Matt's imaginary rescue.

"If word of our existence leaks to the outside world *again*, we'll have to leave this place forever. Move the Vampire Cave to another location."

Hagerty circled Matt as though circling his prey. "Miss Rosie knows about the cave now. She cannot leave. She can *never* leave."

Stay calm, Kubat, he told himself. *Play your next card.*

"But Rosie doesn't have a *clue* where she is, or what's happening, or who you REALLY are." Matt paused for effect. "Go on, ask her."

Hagerty studied Rosie. Matt wondered how he could *not* be attached to this child who adored him so openly.

"Well, Miss Rosie? Do you know where you are?"

Rosie planted a fist on each hip. "We're playing a game," she snipped. "You're It, and you've tagged us and taken us to Wonderland."

Laughter rippled through the dank air.

Hagerty grinned.

Matt gasped.

He'd never seen the man grin before. Two teeth grew longer than the others. Grew into two sharp points. Definitely fangs. Vampire fangs.

Swallowing his apprehension, Matt continued his quest to set his sister free. "See? Rosie just thinks you're playing a game with her."

Hagerty knelt in front of Rosie so he could speak to her eye to eye. "Is it true, child? Do you believe this is simply a game?"

"Yes."

"Well, then, that changes everything." Rising, Hagerty headed back into the shadows for another consultation with his peers.

"But my brother told me different," Rosie blurted.

Hagerty froze to listen.

Rosie stood tall, like she had an important message to give. "Matt said you're not my friend.

He said I can't trust you. He said you're a mean person who'll make us miss Thanksgiving dinner with Grandma."

Oh, geez. Matt's brilliant plan swirled down the drain. He slouched against a wall. *We're doomed. We're definitely doomed.*

Hagerty stepped back into the light. Without missing a beat, he said, "Then again, maybe I *have* done the right thing by bringing both of you here to Wonderland."

Heated opinions skittered across the cavern.

"Wicked!" Hagerty snarled, making Matt flinch.

A young vampire leaped into the light. "Yes, M'lord."

"Lock our prisoners in the deepest, darkest chamber."

Hagerty snapped his fingers. Another door slid open.

The vampire named Wicked nudged Matt and Rosie across the chamber and out the door.

"Lock our prisoners in the deepest, darkest chamber" played over and over in Matt's ears as he stumbled down an earthen corridor with Rosie grasping frantically at his jacket.

10.
Prisoners!

Matt felt like a mouse, scurrying along dark tunnels, lit by that odd red glow. Their escort (guard?) moved quickly, as though used to the twists and turns of the underground pathway.

They were dropping deeper into the earth. Matt could tell by the slant of the dirt floor. Ten-foot doors lined the corridors. He wondered if they were rooms for vampires in transit.

Rosie stumbled.

Matt reached behind to catch her before she fell.

Wicked stopped to wait for them. "Keep up!" he ordered in a threatening tone.

Matt took Rosie's hand to help her walk faster. "She's only six," he shot back, anger heating his neck. The vampires could rough *him* up, but they'd better leave his little sister alone.

Wicked stepped close and whispered, "Forgive me, I have to yell at you in case anyone is listening. I do apologize, but this will be much less painful if you move along quickly so I don't have to shout again."

Huh? Matt was stunned. An apology? From a vampire named Wicked? "Why are you — ?"

"Hush!" Wicked hissed. "Please play along. Act frightened. Act positively terrified of me. It will look so good on my record."

In the red glow, the young vampire's pale face reflected such a pathetic look, Matt felt sorry for him. "Well, okay."

"Off to your doom!" Wicked shouted, so close to Matt's ear it hurt.

Matt dearly hoped he meant "room," not "doom." Playing along, he moaned, "Oh, help! What will happen to us?" Putting fear into his voice was easy since he was already petrified. "Please don't hurt us, Wicked!"

Caped, shadowy figures passed in the tunnel just as Matt shouted.

Wicked punched a fist into the air, obviously pleased.

"Hey!" Rosie called. "Why did that guy ask us to play pretend and act scared?"

Oops.

Matt pulled her close and whispered into her ear. "Play along, Sis. He seems friendly. Maybe he'll help us. Just do what he asks."

Rosie's blaring question had made Wicked pause mid-tunnel to bang his head against the wall in frustration. The sight was both funny and pitiful.

Down, down they trudged. Matt sensed they were going in circles. Were the tunnels shaped like a giant corkscrew?

In the middle of a hairpin curve, Wicked stopped. Pulling keys from his cape, he unlocked a door and herded them in. After a quick glance up and down the tunnel, he stepped inside and closed the door.

The musty chamber was tiny — and pitch-black. "No sense leaving it this way," Wicked muttered, "although they meant for me to." He adjusted something near the door. Dim red light blanketed the room so they could see. Cots lined two walls. That was it for furniture.

"I'm sorry to have to bring you to this miserable place." Wicked wrung his thin, pale hands. "I think they should treat guests a little nicer, but then, they're supposed to be, you know, *scary*."

The vampire reached for the door latch.

"Wait!" Matt cried. "Tell us more. How can we escape?"

Wicked *tsked* and shook his head.

"Yeah," Rosie added. "It's Thanksgiving and Grandma is roasting a turkey for us."

"Turkey?" The vampire's eyes flashed with sudden interest. "How scrumptious."

"With gravy and sweet potatoes with marsh-mallows," Rosie added.

Wicked wrinkled his thin nose. "Well, I don't know about *those* things, but a turkey is quite a treat around here."

Matt knew he meant the *blood* of a turkey — not the *meat*. He wondered if Rosie realized it, too. He also wondered if Mr. Pryor would ever believe what *really* happened to his poor Thanksgiving turkey. . . .

"You're nice," Rosie told him. "But Hagerty was nice, too — at first. Then he turned into a di-aper head."

Diaper head? Was that a bad thing to be in first grade?

Rosie glowered at Wicked. "Are you going to turn into a diaper head, too?"

Bewilderment wrinkled the vampire's brow.

"What she means," Matt explained, "is that you're being too nice to us. Why?"

Crossing the room, Wicked perched on the edge of a cot. "Oh, cobwebs, I *do* try to be mean and nasty, but it just isn't in me. When I received my vampire name, they chose a synonym of evil. A strong, terrifying name for me to live up to."

He motioned them close and dropped his voice. "I'll tell you a little secret. The more frightening a vampire's name, the more harmless he is. That's why Hagerty doesn't have a scary name.

He doesn't *need* one because he's . . . well, he's *beyond* scary. He's bad. He's evil. He's cruel. Plus, he has no sense of humor."

Wicked cracked his knuckles and sighed in disgust. "I hate to trash the man, but he has no sense of fashion, either. Take the white streak in his hair. With a bit of charcoal from burnt elm root, he could cover it in an instant. Makes him look *much* older than his five hundred years."

Matt swallowed a laugh since Wicked sounded sincere. "So," he began, trying to understand what the vampire was telling him. "Your name is frightening, and you're supposed to live up to it?"

"Yes, and I do try," he said. "Didn't I do a splendid job of yelling at you in the tunnel? Oh-ho, that was good." He chuckled to himself. "Wait till you meet Sinister. He's a real pussycat."

Noises outside the door made Wicked spring to his feet.

"Pretend to be scared!" he pleaded.

"Stop!" Matt shouted, playing along. "No! Please!"

Rosie giggled.

Matt pinched her arm to make her stop laughing.

"Ouch!" she hollered.

Wicked smiled, pleased with their acting.

He listened at the door. "They're gone," he

whispered. "And I must go, too. Be brave."

"Wait!" Matt lunged against the door to stop the vampire from opening it. "Before you leave, *please* tell us how to get out of here."

Wicked dusted invisible lint off his cape. "Why do prisoners always want to escape?" he asked. "Ho hum."

Matt wondered how many others had been here before them. "One escaped," he ventured. "Tell me how he did it."

Wicked rubbed his angular chin, thinking. "Yes, one *did* escape. Decades ago." Pausing, he squinted at them. "Oh, cobwebs, you're such likable children, I'll give you *one* clue. But Hagerty is already angry today. If he found out I helped you, he'd exile me to some horrid location — like Hawaii, where the sun shines all the time. How dreadful!"

"Why is he angry?" Rosie asked. "Because of us?"

"No, not you. A few recently arrived vampires ate dinner out last night and didn't clean up after themselves. Hagerty made them go outside in broad daylight to take care of it. Almost killed them!"

Rosie looked confused, but Matt knew exactly what Wicked was talking about. The turkey and the goat. He and Rosie had stumbled upon Hagerty overseeing the cleanup operation. *That* explained why the goat disappeared.

Chupacabras — ha! They were *vampires* — *that's* what they were.

"How can Hagerty go out in daylight at all?" Matt asked, wondering how the vampire could hang around Grandma's house, even with dark glasses and gloves.

"His powers are strong," Wicked told them, "and he has far more stamina than most of us. Sometimes he masquerades in public as a . . . well, as a normal person, just to keep tabs on the outside world."

Ah-ha. And that explained Hagerty's job as Grandma's handyman. . . .

Reaching for the hidden dial near the door, Matt adjusted the light a notch brighter to see better. "About that clue you offered to give us, we won't tell Hagerty. We promise." Matt leaned close, waiting for the clue that might save their lives.

"Oh, yes. The question of how one might escape from the cave." Wicked narrowed his eyes at them. "How do you *think* you might escape?"

Matt hoped this wasn't a trick. Taking a deep breath, he simply guessed. "By finding our way up through the tunnels to the main cavern? Then getting on the, um, earth elevator?" He wasn't sure what to call it.

Wicked howled.

Not the reaction Matt had wanted.

"Up? Oh, no. Now *that's* the mistake every-

52

body makes. Except for the one who got away, of course."

Putting the tips of his fingers together, Wicked whispered, "Here's your clue. In a word: *down*. Think *down*, not *up*."

"But — "

The vampire raised a hand. "That's all I can tell you."

Matt's hopes sank even deeper than the underground chamber.

A zillion questions burned in his mind. Surely the tunnels twisted deeper into the earth. If he and Rosie got the *chance* to escape, how could they find their way out?

And, more importantly, how could they *get* the chance to escape?

With a quick, flashy exit, Wicked was gone.

Along with Matt's hope of freedom.

11.
Welcome to the DoubleFang Hotel

Rosie settled onto one of the cots, unzipped her jacket, and pulled out the raggedy stuffed lamb from Grandma's house.

"You *did* bring Lamb Baby?"

She shrugged since her thumb was in her mouth.

Matt watched her.

In the dark, sitting with her knees pulled up and Lamb Baby clutched to her chest, Rosie looked so tiny and innocent.

A wave of big-brother responsibility washed over him. "I've *got* to get us out of here," he muttered into the darkness.

Plan A: Sit beside Rosie and suck his own thumb. (Where was Wiggly Walrus when you needed him?)

Grow up, Kubat, Matt chided himself.

I'll grow up later, he shot back. *Right now, I need HELLLLLLP!*

He yelled inwardly to keep from sending Rosie into hysterics.

Plan B. . . . Well, what *was* Plan B?

Down, Wicked had said. *Not up.*

Sounded simple — yet it bucked his logical instinct to —

Thomp! Thomp!

The muffled knock startled both of them. Had Wicked come back to help? Or . . . ?

The hinges squeaked as the door flew open and banged against the wall, sending clumps of dirt cascading to the floor.

A shadowy form filled the doorway.

Rosie let out a scream, muffled by her thumb.

Matt stood tall, trying not to let his fear show.

The vampire stepped into the light. Hagerty! His long hair was neatly combed; the white streak perfectly in place.

Seeing the streak reminded Matt of Wicked's words: "Makes him look much older than his five hundred years."

You're standing in a room with a five-hundred-year-old vampire! his mind screamed.

Yikes! Tell me about it.

Striding across the chamber, Hagerty pivoted, his cape swirling around his legs. Touring the prison cell, he stopped near the door to dim the light, making it hard to see.

Rosie didn't speak to Hagerty, which pleased

Matt. Finally, she'd learned the truth about Grandma's handyman.

Matt held his ground in the middle of the chamber and glared at the vampire.

Hagerty dismissed him with a flip of his glove. "It's *your* fault you're here, lad; don't go blaming me."

"My fault?"

"If you hadn't gone looking for the Vampire Cave, I would have left you alone to enjoy the holiday at your grandmother's house."

"Gone looking? Wait a minute. We weren't looking for the cave. We were playing chase."

Hagerty sneered at him. "You expect me to fall for that again? Merely playing a game — posh!"

"But it *was* a game," Rosie insisted. "We — "

"Silence! I wasn't born yesterday, child. Not even the day before. I've been here longer than Thorndale. Longer than your entire country."

"Wow, you're *old*," Rosie exclaimed.

Matt cringed.

With an indignant "Ha-rumph!" the vampire paced across the chamber. "Now that you children are here with us, we have to decide what to *do* with you."

Uneasiness crept over Matt. "But, sir, you can, um, swear us to secrecy, then set us free. We won't breathe a word of this to — "

Hagerty's booming laughter trembled the

walls. "You want me to set you free? You expect me to believe you'd keep the Vampire Cave a secret? Oh, that's amusing. Wait till I tell the boys."

The boys?

"Who would believe us?" Matt insisted. "No one. Not our parents. The police. The FBI. That's why your secret is safe with us."

Hagerty put two fingers on Matt's chest and shoved him backward.

He landed on a cot.

"You can *never* leave the Vampire Cave. For any reason. This is my final decision. What we will *do* with you is another question. You might be put to work, or you might be, well, put to even better use. We'll see."

Matt's legs turned into wobbly licorice sticks, making him glad he was sitting down.

"Diaper head!" Rosie jeered.

"Hush!" Matt hissed. Hagerty held their very lives in his gloved hands. Insulting him was the wrong thing to do.

"Excuse me, Miss Rosie?"

Matt slid to the next cot and clamped a hand over his sister's mouth. "Nothing," he said.

Hagerty stepped close, but it was too dark to read his face. "Miss Rosie, I *do* find you quite charming. And your trust in me has *not* gone unnoticed. Do not let your brother sway you. I am a fabulous handyman with a heart of gold."

His words would have been more convincing if they hadn't been punctuated with a "Heh, heh, heh."

"Matter of fact," Hagerty continued, "you, Miss Rosie, I wouldn't mind keeping around. I always dreamed I'd have a daughter of my own someday." Sentimentality dripped from his words.

Matt imagined going home and telling everyone Rosie had gotten a job as Dracula's daughter. Wouldn't *that* go over big in Thorndale? Ha!

Hagerty took hold of Matt's jacket and yanked him to his feet. "On the other hand," he snarled, "your brother seems to be a troublemaking knave. Maybe our decision about the two of you will be easier than I thought."

Matt prayed Rosie would hold her tongue. *When someone as powerful as Hagerty is deciding your fate, the less said, the better.*

Hagerty started to leave, then paused. "Hungry?" he asked.

"Yes, sir," Matt answered.

"Well, I *did* promise I'd have you in for lunch. So sorry you misinterpreted my words. (Chuckle, chuckle.) I'll see if we have any kind of food that might appeal to you, er, humans."

The slamming door peeled a layer of dirt off the wall.

Feeling his way across the chamber, Matt located the hidden dial that controlled the lights.

He twirled it until the scarlet glow lit each dark corner of the chamber.

Much better.

"I don't like Hagerty anymore," Rosie whined, giving Matt her best pout.

"Well, *now's* a fine time to decide." He knew he sounded gruff, but he didn't care. "If only you'd figured that out sooner, we wouldn't be here. Trapped forever in a Vampire Cave with no way out."

Rosie's bottom lip began to quiver. She looked so pitiful, Matt felt sorry for what he'd said.

Picking up Lamb Baby, he danced the animal across the cot. "Hi, Rosie," he ba-a-a-ed in his best lamb-voice. "Wanna play a game?"

It won him a smile from Rosie.

But didn't make *him* feel better at all.

12.
Wicked and Sinister

Moments later, Wicked entered the chamber. A covered platter of food was balanced on one shoulder. Behind him came another vampire, lugging a folding table.

"This is Sinister," Wicked announced. "My brother."

Quickly setting up the table, Sinister positioned it with great care in front of the prisoners. He reached inside his cape, whisked out a black cloth, and smoothed it onto the table top.

Then he stepped back, let out an ear-splitting lion roar, flapped his cape like wings, and gnashed his teeth — all the while giving Matt and Rosie a superb shot of his glistening fangs.

Rosie cowered, trying to hide behind her brother on the cot.

Matt watched, feeling confused. Wasn't Sinister the one Wicked had called a pussycat?

"Are they gone?" Sinister asked.

Wicked peeked into the corridor. "Gone." He

closed the door and snickered. "That was good, Sin, really good. Almost had *me* scared."

Sinister looked pleased. He bowed before Matt and Rosie. "Begging your pardon, children. Hope I didn't frighten you so badly you can't eat."

Cocking his head, Matt studied the strange brothers. "You two don't really belong here, do you?"

They exchanged glances.

"Not really." Wicked carefully set the platter on the table. "When one is born into a vampire family, one doesn't have a lot of career options. My brother and I would love to fly the coop, but it would be a bit difficult to move into Thorndale and take a job sacking groceries at Food World."

Big sighs from the vampire brothers.

Matt couldn't help but feel sorry for them.

"Yet there's an upside to it," Sinister added. "We will live forever."

"Oh, joy," Wicked muttered, not sounding the least bit joyful.

Sinister moved to the door to listen. "Someone's coming!" He flapped a napkin at Matt and Rosie. "Quick! It's *your* turn to act."

Rosie's screech was so convincing, both vampires flinched in amazement.

"Leave us aloooooooooooone!" Matt hollered. "I'm sooooooo afraid!"

The door swung open.

A monstrous vampire loomed in the tunnel. He

was the meanest one Matt had seen yet. In the red glow, viciousness danced in his eyes.

He regarded his fellow vampires. "Well done, lads. You're really coming along in the torture department. I'll put in a good word to Hagerty for you."

With a cruel laugh aimed at Rosie and Matt, the vampire departed.

"All ri-i-i-i-i-ght!" Sinister quipped, exchanging high fives with his brother. "Thank you *so* much," he added to the prisoners.

"Our pleasure," Matt answered politely — although inside he was thinking *This is too bizarre!* "Would you like us to scream again?"

"Oh, no." Wicked peeked out the door, glancing up and down the passageway. "He's gone now. And to be perfectly honest, people's screams of terror do *not* delight me like they do the others."

Removing covered dishes of food from the platter, he arranged them on the table in front of Matt and Rosie. "By the way, you just met one of the most powerful vampires here, second only in command to Hagerty."

"What's his name?" Matt asked.

"Loman."

Loman? Seemed harmless enough. Then Matt remembered the naming rule. *The more frightening a vampire's name, the more harmless the vampire.* Now he could see why their guards had such frightening names — they were wimps!

"Are you two here all the time?" Matt asked, puzzled. "I thought the Vampire Cave was a stopover for those coming and going."

"We are staff," Wicked explained. "As are Loman and Hagerty. All others check in and out as they travel the world, spreading ill will and havoc wherever they go."

Ewwww.

Sinister lifted the empty platter and opened the door. *"Bon appétit!"* he cried. "Enjoy!"

After a bone-rattling growl, Wicked added, "My children, you are doomed! DOOMED, I SAY!"

Snickering like a couple of kindergartners, they tripped out the door.

Geez. Matt wished all vampires were this harmless.

Yet he had a sinking feeling the Vampire Cave contained far more Lomans and Hagertys than it did Wickeds and Sinisters. . . .

13.
A Peck on the Neck

Rosie lifted covers off the lunch plates. "Wow. They brought us peanut butter sandwiches, pretzels, and grapes." She held a cookie up to the light to see it better. "Look, Matt. Cookies in the shape of turkeys."

Pausing, she bit off the turkey's iced head. "What's in the thermos?"

Matt unscrewed the lid and poured liquid into two cups Wicked had set on the table. "It's milk."

"They eat just like us," Rosie exclaimed, taking a sip.

"I-don't-think-so," Matt singsonged.

Still, the sight of normal food confused him. Where had the vampires gotten people lunch? He doubted the Vampire Cave contained a kitchen that catered to human prisoners.

Too tired and hungry to ponder the oddity, Matt wolfed down his sandwich and dessert. Moving to the other cot, he stretched out to think.

Rosie was still nibbling turkey cookies.

"Okay, Sis, it's time to come up with a plan of escape."

She mumbled an answer with her mouth full.

"We were on the hill above the bridge when we fell into the pit. I wish I knew how far we dropped in the earth elevator." He sighed, wishing he'd paid closer attention while it was all happening. "I think we walked through tunnels for at least five minutes."

Matt closed his eyes to picture the passageways. Even if they escaped from their prison cell, he still didn't know whether to go up or down. Was a vampire clue to be trusted?

The words UP and DOWN floated through his brain, like a video game. UP shot at DOWN, then DOWN lasered UP, exploding the letters into tiny pieces floating off into the atmosphere.

"Sis?" Matt began. Better discuss both plans of escape with Rosie — just in case the chance came to them.

She didn't answer.

Raising onto his elbows, Matt squinted across the dark chamber. She was sound asleep on her cot.

He fell back. *Why do I have to be the oldest? Why do I have to make all the decisions?*

Matt started to replay their options in his mind, but the combination of a full tummy and the darkness soon made him doze.

In his dream, the latch on the door shifted.

Squeeeeeaaaaak! went the hinges.

Was it Hagerty? Coming to inform them of their fate?

Or Wicked? Coming to take away lunch dishes and the table.

He hoped it was the latter.

But what stepped into the chamber was taller than Wicked. Taller than Loman. Taller even than Hagerty.

What stepped into the chamber actually waddled in, filling the entire room with its threatening presence.

Matt opened his mouth to scream, but his terror was drowned by:

"GOBBLE! GOBBLE! GOBBLE!"

Gasping, Matt cowered against the wall.

What stood before him was a turkey. An *enormous* turkey.

A vampire turkey.

The bird's eyes shone pure evil. Two burning spheres threw fiery sparks into the chamber as the horrible feathered thing glowered at Matt.

Its beak and plumage were as black as vampire boots. The fleshy skin on its neck was blood-red, like its eyes.

While Matt watched, the menacing fowl spread its wings and tail feathers until it looked as if it were wearing a cape. A vampire cape.

The nightmare bird parted its beak. Fangs appeared, glowing white in the dark chamber, making Matt flinch.

He stared, watching the fangs lengthen until they grew longer than the bird's beak.

"GOBBLE! GOBBLE! GOBBLE!"

Waddling closer, the turkey prepared to attack.

"IT'S GOING TO PECK MY NECK!" Matt screamed. Out loud this time.

His eyes flew open.

Rosie was shaking him. "What's wrong? What happened?"

"Is it gone?" Matt was afraid to look behind her.

Rosie twirled around. "Who?"

Ohhhhhhhh. Matt sat up and held his head in both hands. *What a nightmare.*

"Did you see a ghost?" Rosie whispered, wide-eyed.

Matt chuckled, now feeling embarrassed. "More like a . . . a poultry-geist." He groaned at his own joke.

"You can borrow Lamb Baby." Rosie lovingly placed her stuffed animal on the cot next to her brother. "He'll watch over you while you nap."

"Thanks." Matt was touched that she would actually give up her lamb. "But now's no time for naps," he told her. "We've got to get out of here."

Rosie hugged Lamb Baby, acting glad that she didn't have to give him up after all. "Do you think we've missed Thanksgiving dinner?" She sounded on the verge of tears.

Matt squinted at the ceiling, trying to calculate the passage of time. "No. We stumbled into the pit around lunchtime, so it must be about mid-afternoon now."

He studied Rosie's pouty face, outlined against the dark wall by the red glow. How could he promise her they'd get home in time for dinner? How could he promise her they'd get home at all?

A sudden loud rapping shot them both to their feet.

What now?

They'd been locked up. And fed. The only thing left was their sentence. Were they doomed to spend eternity in the Vampire Cave?

Matt was afraid to guess beyond that.

Watching the latch lift, he only hoped one thing:

Whatever came through the door — let it NOT be a gobble-roaring, terri-feathering, vampire dream turkey. . . .

14.
A Hundred Days of Thanksgiving

"FEE FI FO FI-ULD!" yelled a frightening voice. "I SMELL THE BLOOD OF A HU-MAN CHI-ULD!"

Uh-oh. Matt's heart began to pound.

The door burst open and in swept Wicked and Sinister.

"How was that?" teased Sinister. "Was I scary enough?"

Wicked shoved him aside in exasperation. "It's Fee Fi Fo *FUM*, little brother, not *Fi-uld.*"

Sinister shoved back. "Well, I had to make it rhyme."

The sight of two vampires bickering over a nursery rhyme almost made Matt laugh. Almost, because he was too nervous about the reason for their visit to be amused.

Were he and Rosie being taken away? To their doom?

Matt stepped in front of his sister to protect her. "Wh-what do you want now?"

"We brought your prison garb," Wicked explained. "We must confiscate your clothes, the contents of your pockets, and, oh yes, that adorable lamb chop."

Rosie gasped. "No! You can't take Lamb Baby. I won't let you."

The image of a thirty-pound first-grader not letting two towering vampires take something away was pretty brave, Matt thought.

"Heavens to cobwebs." Sinister slumped onto a cot and folded his hands between his knees. "I really hate this part, big brother. I'm quite fond of this lad and lass. They deserve to . . . well . . . go on with their lives in a normal sort of way."

Yes! echoed Matt, although he thought it best not to speak.

Wicked's expression softened. "It would be nice. . . ." His voice trailed off. "However . . ."

Distract them! Matt's mind urged. *Make them forget why they're here.* "Um, I have a question," he began, even though he didn't.

Matt's brain whirred, trying to think of a topic that might divert them.

Chupacabras popped into his mind, right on cue.

The vampires (and Rosie) waited for his question.

"There's a legend outside, um, I mean, out in

the world. About something called a *chupa-cabra.*"

"Ho!" laughed Wicked, elbowing his brother. "This one knows his legends, no?"

Sinister snickered accordingly, leaning close to Matt. "What do you know about these *chu-pacabras?*"

Matt reared back, bumping into Rosie, who'd stuffed Lamb Baby out of sight inside her jacket.

"Well, it's a mystery, really." Matt was unsure how much to tell. "Small animals have been found with, um, their blood drained, and, um, fang marks on their necks, but no other marks on their bodies."

Rosie sucked in a breath. "Lamb Baby," she sputtered.

Matt was impressed that she'd connected the dead goat with what he was saying.

"Yes, yes, go on," Sinister urged.

"That's all I know — except for the fact that all this seemed to start in Puerto Rico."

The vampire brothers winked at each other.

"Of course," Sinister said, "Puerto Rico. That's the location of another Vampire Cave, and — "

"Hush, Sin!" rasped Wicked. "You're telling too much."

Sinister's lower lip quivered — a lot like Rosie's did when Matt hurt her feelings.

Wicked wagged a finger at his brother. "Watch

what you say to the prisoners. Do you want to remain an errand boy forever? Our promotions are due, remember? Think before you speak!"

Sinister twisted the hem of his cape, looking truly sorry. "Oh, Wick, you're absolutely right. I forgot about our promotions. Let's get on with it."

Rising, he faced Matt and Rosie. "Go to it, now," he growled. "Off with your clothes. Change into these." He thrust gray, limp garments at them.

Matt's brain warped forward, trying to come up with a way to —

"Wanna play a game?" Rosie blurted.

"Oh, I *love* games," Sinister gushed. "We *never* get to play games anymore — once we pass our first hundred years."

Matt peered at his sister. What was she doing?

"This is a singing game," she explained. "You two sit on the cot and I'll teach it to you."

Matt watched the vampires obey his sister, eagerly taking their places. He seized the opportunity to move as close as he could to the open door without looking too suspicious.

"Here's how it goes." Rosie stationed herself in front of them and began to sing:

> "On the first day of Thanksgiving,
> My grandma gave to me
> A turkey stuffed with herbal dressing."

Matt chuckled. Must be a song she'd learned at school.

"On the second day of Thanksgiving,
my grandma gave to me,
two pumpkin pies,
and a turkey stuffed with herbal dressing."

"Oh, I get it!" Wicked exclaimed. "Let *me* try."
"No, no, let *me* try!" Sinister playfully punched his brother. "I've got something *better*." Clearing his throat, he began:

"On the first day of Thanksgiving,
my vampire gave to me,
a ticket home to Transylvania."

"Ohhhhh, Sin, a ticket home!" Wicked placed two gloved hands over his heart. "You're gonna make me cry."
"Then listen to this," beamed Sinister:

"On the second day of Thanksgiving,
my vampire gave to me,
two pointy fangs, and — "

"A ticket home to Transylvania," finished Wicked, waving his arms as though he were conducting an orchestra.

Delighted, the vampire brothers applauded themselves.

An exasperated Rosie crossed her arms in a huff. "That's *not* the way my song goes."

Matt yanked her to his spot by the door. "Be quiet, Sis. Let them sing it anyway they want. It'll take their minds off us."

"Oh, lass," Sinister called. "How many days of Thanksgiving are there?"

Rosie looked pleased they'd turned to her for the answer. "There are twel — "

"A hundred!" Matt cried. "A hundred days of Thanksgiving."

"Splendid," Sinister chirped. "Oh, this game is *so* fun. But I think we need to add a dance to the lyrics. A Thanksgiving dance."

He pulled Wicked to his feet. Facing each other, the brothers stood tall and bowed regally, forcing Rosie and Matt even closer to the doorway.

Then the two began to twirl in a dance Matt had never seen.

"My turn with the song!" Wicked exclaimed, spinning in a perfect pirouette.

"On the third day of Thanksgiving,
my vampire gave to me . . ."
(Step, kick, twirl his cape, bow, clap, clap.)
"Three hungry bats,

two pointy fangs,
and a ticket home to Transylvania."

Matt held his breath, watching the strange dance of the vampire brothers.

Wicked and Sinister became totally caught up in the game. When they got to the fifth day of Thanksgiving (five mo-l-l-l-ldy rolls), Matt and Rosie quietly slipped out the door.

15.
One Chance in a Zillion

R osie dashed up the tunnel.

"No," hissed Matt, trying to keep his voice low. "*This* way."

Rosie crinkled her face, like she thought he was goofing on her.

"Wicked told us to go *down*, remember?"

She remembered. Making a U-turn, Rosie pounded after him, deeper into the vampire cave.

Going *down* went against Matt's survival instincts. Yet, he kept running, taking every bend of the corridor so fast he had to hold out both arms to keep from slamming into the walls on tight curves.

Then his conscience kicked in.

Why are you trusting a vampire? What if he lied to you in case you escaped? Maybe he knew you'd descend so deeply into the maze of tunnels, you'd never find your way out.

Matt listened to his inner logic. Still, he ran, glancing behind to make sure Rosie followed.

Maybe this *was* a trick. Maybe Wicked *wanted* them to slip out the door.

The vampire said he didn't have it in him to be mean and nasty. By lying, he paved the way for them to run to their *own* doom — then he could wash his hands of their demise.

Would they fall into another pit? Around the next corner? A bottomless pit this time?

Stop it, Kubat. The vampire brothers have been nothing but kind to you. Why would they deceive you?

For their promotions.

Oh, yeah.

The air was getting fresher, which also bucked Matt's logic. Seemed like the deeper they ran, the more stifling the air should become. Clammy, musty, dank, stale. How could fresh air find its way this deep underground?

The corridor twisted and turned, but no doors lined these walls. Did the vampires inhabit only the upper rooms?

Matt ran on. With every footfall, a question hammered through his mind: *How can DOWN be the way out?*

Go back, his mind warned.

Rosie is trusting you to save her, and —

"Halt!" boomed a mighty voice.

Terror streaked through Matt. They'd been caught! He threw a hurried glance over one shoulder without missing a step.

Three vampires chased after them.

Angry, fierce-looking vampires.

Something told Matt these guys meant business. They looked heartless. Devious. Dangerous.

Their names must be way mild. Like Moe, Larry, and Curly.

"Run!" shrieked Rosie.

Exactly what Matt was doing.

Rounding the next corner, he discovered the reason for the fresher air. Daylight! They'd come to another cave entrance. The back door, perhaps? The way the vampires entered?

"Burn, Rosie, we're almost out!"

Her howl told him something had gone wrong.

Slamming against a wall to stop, Matt twirled.

Rosie stood frozen in the tunnel. "I-I dropped Lamb Baby!" she cried.

The sound of pounding boots told Matt it was now or never to get out into the daylight that would save them.

Rushing back to his sister, he grabbed her wrist.

"No!" she cried.

"I'll buy you another Lamb Baby," Matt shouted. "I'll buy you a *zillion* Lamb Babies. Just come *on.*"

She tugged away from him. "I'll be quick."

"No, Rosie, they're after us!"

On cue, the vampires rounded the last corner and barreled toward them.

"Now's our only chance!" Hoisting her into his arms, he bolted toward the light.

Pale, bony fingers reached out for them, making Rosie scream in Matt's ear. Her screams mingled with his own.

He tore through a bramble hedge, ripping his jacket as he burst outside. Stumbling over rocks, he kept on running.

They were in a ravine.

Blinking at the sudden brightness, Matt tried to scramble up the side of the gorge, but Rosie was too heavy to carry.

He let her slide to the ground. Then he dared a glance behind.

Bushes almost hid the entrance to the cave. But Matt could plainly see, huddled in the dark, the outline of three forms, shielding their eyes.

"We made it!"

Part of him wanted to dance in front of his undead audience and jeer, "Nyah, nyah, nyah!" But another part wanted to make darn sure they were well out of danger.

Grabbing Rosie's hand, he hustled up the hill. At the top, he pivoted, trying to get his bearings.

"A road!" she yelped, tearing down the other side.

She was right. Through the trees below, he could plainly see a road. And up ahead, a bridge. Was it the road to Grandma's house?

Matt dashed after his sister. Probably didn't

need to run anymore, yet he wasn't going to feel safe till they made it back to Grandma's.

Besides, late afternoon shadows darkened the forest. The overcast sky was milky gray, promising snow tonight. The last thing Matt wanted was to be out here after dark. No way would they get away from creatures of the night then. *Yikes.*

Making it to the road, they slowed to catch their breath, walking fast to the bridge. Matt read the sign, "Hazard Creek. This is the way we came in! Should be one more bridge, then the turnoff on Calumet. Let's hustle; we've still got a long hike."

Matt was exhausted. He could have curled up on the side of the road and taken a nap. But he pushed on. Up the gravelly road.

Hurry, hurry, hurry! his mind warned.

"There's the last bridge!" Rosie cried.

Knowing the turnoff was on the other side flooded relief over him. They were going to make it. Hooray!

He grinned at Rosie, but her wounded expression told him she was still miffed about the demise of Lamb Baby.

He reached to tickle a smile out of her, but a sudden eerie noise — loud enough to pain his ears — stopped him cold.

The soft twilight air exploded with a million

shrill whines. A high-pitched shrieking kind of whine.

Rosie froze in fear. Her gaze locked with Matt's. "W-what's that?"

Matt was afraid to turn around.

But he did.

Behind them, rising over the hill, floated an ominous black cloud.

Confused, Matt squinted at the sky. The sudden realization of what he was witnessing rolled a tidal wave of terror through him.

"Ohmigosh!" he stammered. "Bats!"

Not only bats, his panicked mind screamed. *VAMPIRE BATS . . . !*

16.
Flying Vampires!

Shock buckled Matt's legs.
Crumbling onto the road, he rolled over and gaped at the unearthly sight of the shadowy forms rising over the horizon.

His heart pounded so fiercely, he almost couldn't hear Rosie screaming at him. "Get up! Get up! Get up!"

For some reason, his fear of the bats burned stronger than his fear of the vampires themselves.

These ARE *the vampires, Kubat, only in another form.*

Flying vampires.

EEEEEEEEEEEEEEEEEEEEEEEEE!

The squeals mingled with equally loud squeals coming from Rosie.

Survival overruled Matt's fear. Springing to his feet, he grabbed her hand and raced the last few yards to the bridge.

Sliding down an embankment to the stream, he yanked Rosie safely beneath the bridge.

"Listen to me!" Matt heard the tremble in his own voice. He'd never been this scared in his entire life.

"Bats find their, um, prey by radar," he huffed, trying to get the words out and make sense of what he'd seen. "Echoes bounce back to them so they can track the movements of their, um, target. If we stay hidden under the bridge, the bats can send out all the radar they want and never detect us."

Matt hoped his logic worked. The radar tidbit was actually the only thing he knew about bats, remembered from fourth-grade science class.

Rosie stood like a statue, eyes wide, listening. "But I wanna go home."

"So do I," Matt whispered. "So do I."

The low bridge wouldn't allow him to stand. Moving up close to the embankment hid them from view on the sides, thanks to the bridge's metal supports. Still, he thought it best if they didn't move at all.

"Come up here and sit down, Rosie. We need to stay perfectly still."

He watched tears trickle down her face as she obeyed him. She was a lot braver than he'd expected. Made him proud — even though she usually drove him crazy.

"We're almost home," he said to comfort her. "We just have to wait till the coast is clear."

Times like this, he wished he had a cellular phone like Mom's. All he'd have to do is dial Grandma's number, then Dad would come barreling down here in the Jeep and rescue them.

A soft flapping of leathery wings told Matt the vampire bats were flying over the bridge. He held his breath. As long as they stayed underneath it, they *should* be okay.

The two settled in. Listening to the stream burble was soothing, even though the calming sound was interrupted periodically by bat shrieks and flutterings.

"I'm hungry," Rosie muttered.

"I know. So am I." Matt wondered what time it was and how long they should wait before making a run for it. If he remembered correctly, Grandma's house wasn't far up the rutted road. Yet, all it would take is one bat to pick them up on radar, and . . .

"Do you think Wicked and Sinister will get into trouble?" Rosie asked. "I mean, because of us?"

That notion had been wandering through Matt's mind. He liked the bumbling vampire brothers and really wished them no ill will.

"Mmm, don't know," he answered. "From what Wicked said, they could be banished to some horrid place, sunny and bright."

"How awful for them," Rosie teased, making a goofy face through her tears. "Hey, Matt, wanna sing a song?" she asked. "Or play a game?"

He gaped at her. How could she think of anything other than surviving the next ten minutes? "No songs. No games," he told her. "I think we need to be extra quiet."

The instant he said it, Matt realized that songs and games might be how first-graders handled stress.

On that thought, he relented, to keep her entertained. "If I play a game with you, will you forgive me about Lamb Baby?"

She stayed quiet, fiddling with her shoelaces.

He nudged her. "How about making up more verses for the Vampire Song? Like, six could be . . ." He paused to think. "On the sixth day of Thanksgiving, my vampire gave to me six sturdy coffins. La la la la la. And a ticket home to Transylvania."

Rosie laughed. "I know what seven can be. Seven swirly capes."

"Good!"

She giggled. "You do eight."

"Mmm." Combining Thanksgiving and vampires in his mind was just as odd as combining grandmothers and jogging. "How about eight departed turkeys?"

"Ewww," Rosie groaned.

As Matt paused to think up something good

for nine, he noticed how quiet it had become. Too quiet, actually. No wind. No birds. No bat noises.

Leaning around the metal bridge supports, he peeked at the sky. Dusk was settling over the land, but snow clouds kept the sky light. No sign of bats in any direction.

They could be lurking in the trees.

I know. But if we stay here any longer, night will fall and we'll run into more than bats.

The thought of coming face-to-face with Hagerty, who'd told them they could *never* leave the Vampire Cave, made Matt's blood turn to ice.

"I can't think of anything for the ninth day of Thanksgiving," Rosie said.

"We'll finish the song later," Matt told her. "Are you ready to make a run for it?"

She whimper-yelped in answer.

So, she was just as frightened as he was — even though he'd tried to hide it.

Standing hunched over, Matt pulled Rosie to her feet. "We either sit under this bridge all night, or we go home for Thanksgiving dinner. What's it gonna be?"

"Turkey."

"Yes, perfect. Think turkey. Think it harder than you've ever thought anything before. Picture it roasted golden. Smell it steaming from the oven. Taste the juicy meat. And keep running. No matter what happens, don't stop until you're safe inside Grandma's house."

"Okay. But I wish I had Lamb Baby. . . ."

He squeezed her hand in sympathy. "Don't make any noise until the house is in sight," he warned. "Then, if you feel like yelling, be my guest."

She nodded.

"Let's go."

Shivering to the bone — from fear as well as the cold night air — he grasped Rosie's elbow to hustle her up the embankment to the road.

Matt was proud of the pep talk he'd given his little sister.

He only wished someone would do the same for him.

17.
A Five-Hundred-Year-Old Bat

Matt's feet pounded up the gravel road. He tried to stay under the canopy of branches, even though most of them were bare.

Dusk made hopping over potholes in the road difficult, but he dodged the ruts as best he could, hoping neither of them twisted an ankle.

Rosie kept up, which surprised Matt. He figured he'd have to end up carrying her again, but she was a faster runner than he'd thought.

"Look!" Matt huffed, out of breath. "There's the house! I can see the chimney above the tree-tops."

"Turkey!" hollered Rosie.

"Turkey is right! We're almost there, Sis. We're going to make it!"

Up, up the road.

In the deepest tunnel of his mind, Matt thought he heard the fluttering of another set of leathery wings.

Please let it be his imagination.

Surely fate wouldn't let them get this close to safety, then trick them — would it?

The fluttery noise grew louder.

Noooooooo!

"Run, Rosie!" he cried, turning on a burst of speed.

EEEEEEEEEEEEEEEEEEEEEEEEEE!

With a frantic shriek, Rosie bolted ahead.

Matt tore after her, staying on her heels.

Up the driveway. There was the Jeep! And the wooden stairway to the porch. It all looked too familiar for Matt to believe they weren't going to make it.

Rosie's shoes hit the steps seconds before his.

Focusing on the door at the top, he clomped upstairs as fast as his legs would move.

Swwwooooooooosh!

Matt ducked. *Yikes!*

A bat had swooped past, almost clipping his ear with its wings.

Raising his arms, Matt prepared for another attack.

It didn't come.

Grabbing the back of Rosie's jacket, he stopped her mid-step.

Where had the bat gone?

"Look!" Rosie cried.

At the top, hanging from the front porch screen, was the largest, ugliest bat Matt had ever seen. Of course, he'd never seen a real bat before, but he knew they weren't supposed to be as big as baseball mitts.

Hagerty! was all Matt could think.

The Evil Lord of the Vampire Cave.

Blocking their way to safety.

Matt's heart skittered. Why had he thought he could outwit a five-hundred-year-old vampire?

He watched the bat's beady eyes watching him — while his great plan of escape melted away like an oozing layer of marshmallows in a dish of Thanksgiving yams.

18.
Sweeping with the Enemy

The next instant, Grandma Kubat burst out the front door, wielding a broom. "Drat those bats! I've had enough of them hanging on my screens!"

Rosie clutched Matt's arm in shock.

He tried to yell, "Grandma, no!" but it came out a limp whisper.

Matt feared for her safety. How could she know this was no ordinary bat? How could she know it was a Master Vampire? The cruelest creature of the night this side of Transylvania, according to Wicked.

The sight of Grandma in her horn-of-plenty apron whacking at the Bat King would have been funny if Matt hadn't known the rest of the story.

Lunging past Rosie, he took the stairs two at a time and wrenched the broom from his grandmother's grasp.

"Matthew and Rosie! There you are! Your father and I have been worried sick." She reached for the broom but Matt held on to it. "Where've you been? It's almost dark out. Get inside."

"*You* get inside!" Matt insisted.

Rosie understood the danger. Dashing up the steps, she grabbed Grandma's arm and hurried her into the house, holding the screen shut behind them.

Grandma looked bewildered. "What are you kids doing? I'm trying to get that nasty thing off my screen."

Balancing on the top step, Matt swung the broom.

The vampire bat fought back.

Unhooking itself from the screen, it rose up in front of him.

Since when do bats hover? flashed through Matt's mind.

This is no ordinary bat!

The broom became a lance. Matt shoved it into the bat's belly.

The bat recoiled, then attacked, flying at Matt with its claws and jaws wide open.

"Why, I never saw a bat do that before," exclaimed Grandma. "Matthew Kubat, you get in here this instant!"

"I'm trying, Grandma!"

The bat landed on the railing.

Staying on guard, Matt circled slowly, moving closer to the door.

Rosie kept holding the screen shut till he got there.

Good move, he thought. What if the bat flew inside the house? And changed back into Hagerty? Hagerty the vampire — not the handyman. The entire family would be doomed. . . .

The bat's eyes pierced Matt's with a hateful, burning glare.

Suddenly, a multitude of fluttering wings met Matt's ears. He glanced up. The bat cloud was back, flying north, away from Calumet Woods.

EEEEEEEEEEEEEEEEEEEEEEEE!

"They're calling you to come join them."

Matt spat out the words, trying to sound disgusted, but the quiver in his voice gave away his fear.

Trying to keep his hands steady, he held the broom in position to swing again. "Go, Hagerty. You've been found out. You have to leave this place forever. You said so yourself."

Then the bat that was Hagerty made a mistake. He shifted his gaze away from Matt and tilted his furry head. To catch the other bats' radar message?

Matt didn't hesitate. *WHAP!* went the broom, sweeping the monster bat off the railing.

Matt lunged for the door. Rosie let him in, then slammed it shut.

"Well, I never," Grandma muttered, peering out the window.

Matt waited. Seconds later, the giant bat rose up and flew off toward the black cloud, now disappearing over the treetops.

"We won," he whispered to Rosie.

"Merciful heavens!" Grandma *tsked* a few times, then locked the door, which pleased Matt. "I'll have to ask Mr. Pryor how he keeps bats off his screens." She turned toward the kitchen. "Meanwhile, I've got to get dinner on the table. You two go wash up; it's time to eat."

Music to Matt's ears. He started to move away from the window, but Rosie grabbed his sleeve.

"Look!"

He squinted into the dim light. Against the snow-gray sky, two stray bats, yards behind the others, flew in zigzaggy loop-de-loops.

"Do you think?" Rosie began.

"That it's Wicked and Sinister?" Matt finished. "I can't imagine any *other* vampires acting that way, can you?" He chuckled at the weird sight. "Maybe that's their way of telling us they're glad we got away."

Rosie laughed at the bats' antics. "Those two were really nice."

"Nice?" Matt scoffed. "Nice or not, Sis, never forget the truth. They're *still* vampires."

19.
Please Pass the Turkey

Awonderful aroma beckoned to Matt and Rosie, coaxing them to hang up their jackets, wash off dirt from the Vampire Cave, comb their hair, and change into clean clothes.

Matt had one more important task to take care of before he could eat. In the den, he scooped Wiggly Walrus off the sofa bed. Sneaking into Rosie's room, he placed the stuffed walrus on her pillow so she'd find it at bedtime.

Granted, it wasn't a lamb, but it made a warm, cuddly replacement — guaranteed to stave off little-sister nightmares.

In the kitchen, Grandma stood at the counter, surrounded by dishes, pots, and pans. Her hair was coming undone from its butterfly clip, and her face was as pink as the smoked salmon appetizer she was preparing. "I was just telling your father how brave you were out there with that bat, Matthew."

Dad zipped past, carrying dishes to the dining

95

room table. "Hey, you two are in *big* trouble. Your mom called and I had to tell her I didn't know where you were. I was about to send out a posse to search for you."

Matt and Rosie exchanged glances. Seemed like they'd been gone for *days*. And a posse was just what they'd needed — equipped with garlic and mirrors and matches. . . .

"Didn't you look for us at lunchtime?" Rosie asked.

Grandma rinsed her hands and wiped them on her *Let's Talk Turkey* towel. "No. Not after Hagerty told us how much fun you two were having out back, playing hide-and-seek. Sweet of him to wrap up your lunch and take it to you."

Ohhhhhh. That explained the "normal" lunch in the Vampire Cave.

"Let's hustle, kids." Dad handed napkins to Rosie and an ice cube tray to Matt. "Your grandmother needs help."

"Thought she had a handyman," Matt ventured.

"Not anymore." Dad looked relieved.

"What happened to Hagerty?" Rosie asked, sounding innocent.

Grandma began to whip potatoes with a vengeance. "Hagerty up and quit on me this afternoon. Said he was moving on short notice. Short notice — ha! In the middle of dinner preparations?"

Matt clunked ice cubes into glasses and winked at his sister. So, it was true. The vampires *had* been forced to move their cave.

They were gone from Calumet Woods forever. Off to another location, somewhere else in the world.

"Time to eat," Grandma said.

Dad carried the platter of turkey to the table. As they took their places, Grandma raised a glass of apple cider to toast her family. "Happy Thanksgiving, everybody!"

Rosie lifted her glass of milk. "Happy Fangsgiving!" A look of dismay colored her face the same reddish glow as the lights in the Vampire Cave. "Oops!" she cried, while everyone laughed.

Matt clinked his glass against hers, whispering so only she could hear, "Truer words were never spoken."

Then, in a loud voice, he said something he'd been *dying* to say all day: "*Please* pass the turkey!"

THE VAMPIRE THANKSGIVING SONG

On the first day of Thanksgiving,
My vampire gave to me
A ticket home to Transylvania.

On the second day of Thanksgiving,
My vampire gave to me
Two pointy fangs,
And a ticket home to Transylvania.

On the third day of Thanksgiving,
My vampire gave to me
Three hungry bats,
Two pointy fangs,
And a ticket home to Transylvania.

On the fourth day of Thanksgiving,
My vampire gave to me
Four rotten yams,
Three hungry bats,
Two pointy fangs,
And a ticket home to Transylvania.

On the fifth day of Thanksgiving,
My vampire gave to me
Five mo-l-l-l-ldy rolls . . .
Four rotten yams,

Three hungry bats,
Two pointy fangs,
And a ticket home to Transylvania.

On the sixth day of Thanksgiving,
My vampire gave to me
Six sturdy coffins,
Five mo-l-l-l-ldy rolls . . .
Four rotten yams,
Three hungry bats,
Two pointy fangs,
And a ticket home to Transylvania.

On the seventh day of Thanksgiving,
My vampire gave to me
Seven swirly capes,
Six sturdy coffins,
Five mo-l-l-l-ldy rolls . . .
Four rotten yams,
Three hungry bats,
Two pointy fangs,
And a ticket home to Transylvania.

On the eighth day of Thanksgiving,
My vampire gave to me
Eight departed turkeys,
Seven swirly capes,
Six sturdy coffins,

Five mo-l-l-l-ldy rolls . . .
Four rotten yams,
Three hungry bats,
Two pointy fangs,
And a ticket home to Transylvania.

On the ninth day of Thanksgiving,
My vampire gave to me
Nine creepy mansions,
Eight departed turkeys,
Seven swirly capes,
Six sturdy coffins,
Five mo-l-l-l-ldy rolls . . .
Four rotten yams,
Three hungry bats,
Two pointy fangs,
And a ticket home to Transylvania.

On the tenth day of Thanksgiving,
My vampire gave to me
Ten wormy pumpkins,
Nine creepy mansions,
Eight departed turkeys,
Seven swirly capes,
Six sturdy coffins,
Five mo-l-l-l-ldy rolls . . .
Four rotten yams,
Three hungry bats,
Two pointy fangs,
And a ticket home to Transylvania.

On the eleventh day of Thanksgiving,
My vampire gave to me
Eleven horns-of-nothing,
Ten wormy pumpkins,
Nine creepy mansions,
Eight departed turkeys,
Seven swirly capes,
Six sturdy coffins,
Five mo-l-l-l-ldy rolls . . .
Four rotten yams,
Three hungry bats,
Two pointy fangs,
And a ticket home to Transylvania.

On the twelfth day of Thanksgiving,
My vampire gave to me
Twelve strokes of midnight,
Eleven horns-of-nothing,
Ten wormy pumpkins,
Nine creepy mansions,
Eight departed turkeys,
Seven swirly capes,
Six sturdy coffins,
Five mo-l-l-l-ldy rolls . . .
Four rotten yams,
Three hungry bats,
Two pointy fangs,
And a ticket home to Transylvania.

About the Author

Dian Curtis Regan is the author of more than thirty books, including *Home for the Howl-idays*, *The Vampire Who Came for Christmas*, *My Zombie Valentine*, and the *Ghost Twins* series. Ms. Regan is from Colorado Springs and presently lives in Oklahoma City, where she shares an office with a vampire cat (he likes to nip her neck) and eighty walruses, none of whom show vampiric tendencies. (So far . . .)